Silverlake
Fairy School

Bugs and Butterflies

Silverlake Fairy School

A magical world
where fairy dreams come true

Collect the titles in this series:

Unicorn Dreams

Wands and Charms

Ready to Fly

Stardust Surprise

Bugs and Butterflies

Dancing Magic

For more enchanting fairy fun, visit
www.silverlakefairyschool.com

Silverlake Fairy School

Bugs and Butterflies

Elizabeth Lindsay

Illustrated by Anna Currey

USBORNE

For Emma and Kathryn, with love

First published in 2009 by Usborne Publishing Ltd., Usborne House,
83-85 Saffron Hill, London EC1N 8RT, England.
www.usborne.com

Text copyright © Elizabeth Lindsay, 2009

Illustrations copyright © Usborne Publishing Ltd., 2009

A CIP catalogue record for this book is available from the British Library.

UK ISBN 9780746095324 First published in America in 2012 AE.
American ISBN 9780794530662 JFMAMJJ SOND/11 01562/1
Printed in Dongguan, Guangdong, China.

Contents

Chapter One

Practice

Flying her fastest, Lila glimpsed a flash of sky-blue wings from out of the corner of her eye. Bella had almost caught up with her.

"I must somersault!" Lila told herself. "One, two, three, now." And over she went.

"Careful, Lila!" Bella cried. "You're supposed to tap my shoulder with your wand, not dig me in the ribs."

"Sorry," said Lila. "I really didn't mean to."

Today, the Star Clan fairies were having an

Bugs and Butterflies

important training session in the Bugs and Butterflies ring. Every single one of them wanted to be picked to play on the Star Clan team. Bugs and Butterflies was the school game at Silverlake Fairy School and a trophy cup would be presented to the winning clan team at the end of the year.

However, there were many matches to be won or lost before the champions would be decided. The present trophy holders were the fairies of the Sun Clan. But the fairies in the other three clans – Star, Moon and Clouds, were eager to win the cup for themselves. Yet before any of this could happen, the Star Clan team had to be selected and Lila and Bella badly wanted to be chosen.

Bella, one of Lila's two best friends in Charm One, her first year class, was already an expert at the game. She had played for the Star Clan last year and was hoping to keep her place on the team. The first clan matches of the new school

Practice

year were in three days' time, which was why they were practicing so hard.

"I don't think I'm ever going to get the timing right," Lila despaired, checking she hadn't bent the purple star at the tip of her wand.

"Yes, you are," Bella told her firmly. She was teaching Lila a special defensive somersault. "You went over too soon. It's an easy mistake to make when someone's chasing you. Wait a fraction of a second longer. Try again."

One of the Bugs and Butterflies' rules was that if an opposing team member's wand tapped you on the shoulder, you were out and had to leave the game. But it was possible to somersault underneath a chasing fairy and come up behind them instead. This was the defensive somersault Lila was trying to learn.

After three more failures, with Bella again on her tail, Lila rocketed across the sky with extra determination. With her quickest somersault yet, she flipped underneath Bella and finally tapped her friend on the shoulder.

"That's it," beamed Bella, delighted. "That was perfect. Now you've done it once you'll be able to do it again and again. One more time for luck."

Lila flew up into the air hoping she *could* do it again. She dodged several other fairies, until she was really speeding above the Bugs and Butterflies ring. She slowed a little and glanced over her shoulder. Bella was catching up fast. Lila made herself wait until Bella was stretching out with her wand. It was almost a hit. But at the very last second Lila somersaulted. Bella didn't stand a chance. Lila had tapped her shoulder before Bella could even change direction.

"That was the best yet, Lila," Bella grinned. "Perfect timing. You got me out easily. And I really thought you hadn't seen me."

"Ah, but I had," smiled Lila. "I think I've got the knack at last."

Bugs and Butterflies

"You certainly have," said Bella, giving Lila's arm a friendly nudge. "Well done!"

From a spectator's branch at the side of the Bugs and Butterflies ring several Sun Clan fairies were gathering, ready for their turn to practice. Lila couldn't help noticing that Princess Bee Balm and her friend Sea Holly were among them. The Princess was scrutinizing Lila with a calculating gleam and Lila wondered what she was thinking. She didn't want another quarrel with the Princess, but often Bee Balm went out of her way to start one. If only she could forgive me for being a palace kitchen fairy, Lila thought, not for the first time. But so far Bee Balm had shown no intention of doing so. She hated having Lila, a lowly palace servant, in the same class as her royal self.

"Do you know, there's a rumor going around that Bee Balm wants to play on the Sun Clan team?" said Bella, who had also noticed the

Practice

Princess and Sea Holly watching them. "But if I remember correctly, Her Royal Highness is frightened of bugs!"

"Well," said Lila. "She must have overcome her fear. She can be a very determined fairy when she wants to be."

"I wish Meggie could be like that," said Bella. "I tried to persuade her to come to the practice today but she wouldn't."

"Well, if you hadn't told her how vile it is being caught by a podbug, she might have," said Lila.

"Yes, but it doesn't hurt or anything," said Bella. "If you're stupid enough to let one capture you, they just pod you up. It's quite harmless, a little like being wrapped up in paper and tied up with string."

"I don't think Meggie relished the idea of being podded up," laughed Lila. "Even after you explained that another fairy could easily release you. Anyway, she would much rather be doing her sewing. Playing Bugs and Butterflies is too boisterous for Meggie." But it was more than that. In spite of reminding her many times that the magic bugs were harmless, Meggie remained frightened of them. Lila found it a puzzling fear but, unlike Bella, she didn't expect Meggie to lose it so she was able to be more sympathetic.

Once the silver sunflower that started the Bugs and Butterflies game was planted in the middle of the ring, both Lila and Bella shared the same excitement. When the magic began and the sunflower seeds spread across the grass Lila's heart always beat faster. It was amazing to watch the little silver specks turn into the flowers, trees, shrubs, butterflies and bugs that made up the game. But even though Mistress Pipit, their teacher, encouraged everyone to join in, Meggie did so reluctantly and avoided playing altogether if she could.

Practice

"Come on, Lila," said Bella, tugging her friend's arm. "We're being called over."

The players gathered around Musk Mallow, their Head of Star Clan fairy and team captain. Lila folded her wings, her purple coloring vibrant among the chattering group. Indeed, she was the only purple fairy pupil in the whole school. But, and this was something that had always amazed Lila, there *was* one other purple fairy – the only other purple fairy she had ever met – the Headteacher, Fairy Godmother Whimbrel.

"Pay attention everybody," said Musk Mallow, who was holding up her wand for silence. Musk Mallow was the best Bugs and Butterflies player in the Star Clan. Every fairy said so.

"Well done all of you. We have time for one last exercise before we hand over to the Sun Clan. We're now going to put that somersault into practice." Musk Mallow winked at Linnet. Linnet was the Star Clan's second best player; Lila and

Bugs and Butterflies

Bella were agreed about that. With a wave of her wand, Musk Mallow sent a swarm of little blue and green practice stars whizzing into the air. Then she chased several stars and caught and popped them. Linnet chased after her and tried, but failed, to catch her. Musk Mallow somersaulted thrillingly fast. Linnet didn't stand a chance.

"Right, that was a little demonstration of what I want you to do. So, in your pairs, choose one of you to make the stars and the other to be the catcher. Then switch over. Five minutes. Off you go."

"Me first," said Bella, shaking six tiny blue stars into the air with her wand and racing after them. Bella had caught four before Lila was even close. But when Lila did catch up it was easy to tap Bella's shoulder.

"Flustering flutterers," said Bella, as the magic in her two remaining stars ran out and they popped by themselves. "I didn't think you'd catch up to me that quickly."

Practice

"My turn," said Lila, sending a rabble of ten purple stars skyward. She raced after them and had caught one, two, three, four, five stars before Bella was anywhere near her. Lila tapped one final star before she somersaulted. Bella was caught before she knew it.

"Double flustering flutterers," cried Bella. "That was amazing, Lila! You do learn fast."

The five minutes were up and Musk Mallow gathered the Star Clan fairies together again.

"I've been watching some excellent work today," she said. "Especially Lilac Blossom. By the end you were turning some nifty somersaults." Bella gave Lila a nudge. Musk Mallow didn't give praise unless she really meant it. Lila smiled shyly, but inside she was really pleased.

"Now listen carefully, everyone," said Musk Mallow. "I'm going to have a final trial the day after tomorrow, when I will select the team for our first Clan match. The match'll take place the day after. If you want to be picked for the team, don't be late."

Competition to play for the Star Clan team was getting more intense. Lila and Bella had no intention of being late.

The Sun Clan fairies were already spilling into the Bugs and Butterflies ring ready for their training session, Bee Balm and Sea Holly among them.

"Well played, Lilac Blossom," smiled Bee Balm, with a flick of her pink hair. "You're good at somersaults, aren't you? She was, wasn't she, Sea Holly?" Sea Holly gave a little nod and a smirk. "Do you think you'll be picked for the Star's team?" Bee Balm added.

"I'd like to be," said Lila, wondering where this conversation was leading.

"Well, if you keep playing like that you might well be," said the Princess. "May the best players be selected." And, with a swish of her glittering pink frock, she joined the crowd of fairies gathering around Marigold, the Head of Sun Clan fairy.

"What was all that about?" Bella asked.

"No idea," shrugged Lila. "Perhaps she's trying to be nice."

"Oh yeah," said Bella, making a face. "If you believe that you'll believe anything."

"Well, one thing's for sure," said Lila. "If Bee Balm gets picked for the Sun Clan and we get picked for the Star Clan, we'll end up playing against her."

Chapter Two

A Surprise Visit

The two friends walked back to school through the Wishing Wood, too tired to fly, treading the well-worn path between the giant oak trees that would take them to the garden and the entrance to the Hall of Rainbows.

"Bella," said Lila, stopping. "When Bee Balm stares at me like she did when we were practicing I always feel she's plotting something."

"Sizing up the opposition, more like."

"I do wish she and I could get along better. She

A Surprise Visit

never usually speaks to me unless she has to and, now, because she's actually said something nice about my somersaults, I'm feeling suspicious."

"I wouldn't worry about it. If she's being pleasant for once, that's good, isn't it? And if she's plotting, we'll find out soon enough," said Bella.

Lila sat on a tree root to think. Bee Balm had already gotten her into enough trouble with her teacher, Mistress Pipit, this year already.

"The thing is I don't want to disappoint Pipity again," she told Bella. "She's the best teacher in the world."

Bella nodded. "Yup, the best, even though she is a Sun Clan mistress."

"Yes, but she never ever favors the Sun Clan fairies. She's fair and kind and that's why we all adore her," said Lila.

"With the possible exception of Bee Balm who only adores herself," said her friend impishly.

Bugs and Butterflies

"Bella!" said Lila, with a gasp.

"But it's true," said Bella, obstinately.

"Well, I suppose it does often look that way," said Lila, with a relenting grin. Then she was serious again.

"I just wish that Bee Balm and I didn't always end up being rivals."

"Don't even bother thinking about it," said Bella. "It's her problem. *She* makes it like that, not you. Anyway, you're a far better Bugs and Butterflies player than Bee Balm. And you've got more chance of being picked for your team than she does." Bella spun her wand in the air and caught it before sitting down beside Lila.

"I'm so lucky to have you as my friend," Lila said, grinning and making room. "You're good at cheering me up. It's the one reason I'm glad you failed all your charm exams last year. If you hadn't, you'd be one of those awfully grown-up Second Years who don't speak much to Charm

A Surprise Visit

One fairies. Meggie and I would never have gotten to know you so well."

"What do you mean 'gotten to know me so well'?" Bella asked, with a pretend frown. "You haven't found out all my secrets, have you?"

This set Lila chuckling and she said, "Be serious. You don't have any."

"No, I don't," Bella admitted with a grin. "But if I did have I would always share them with you and Meggie."

From the leaves above came a chuck, chuck, chuck, chatter sound and an acorn landed on the ground in front of them. The fairies looked up to see two playful red squirrels sitting side by side on a branch.

"What are you up to, you naughty things?" Lila asked. "Shoo, tufty ears!"

The squirrels dropped two more acorns, flicked their tails and scampered higher up the tree to hide.

Bugs and Butterflies

"We're not chasing you," Bella cried. "We're too tired. You can play on your own."

Lila picked up the three acorns. "I know what we can do with these." She put one in her pocket and touched the other two with the star on the tip of her wand. "Acorn balloons!" she commanded. Bella watched, intrigued, as the acorns filled up with air and grew bigger. They floated gently at nose level.

"Withering wellipedes, that's a clever idea, Lila," she said, leaping onto one. "Can they carry us back to the Star Clan turret?"

"Of course, they're just perfect for tired fairies," said Lila, lying along the length of the other. It was as comfortable as a cushion. With a shake of her wand, the acorn balloons rose, passing alongside the branches of the oak tree. The two squirrels chattered in noisy surprise as the fairies drifted skyward.

They rose high above the Wishing Wood. In one

A Surprise Visit

direction, tall among the trees, they could see the Flutter Tower, where they had their fairy dance and gym lessons, and in the other direction, the school's majestic silver turrets.

"How lucky we are to be at Silverlake Fairy School," said Lila. "A school in a castle! What more could a fairy want?"

The waters of Great Silver Lake, surrounding the castle, glistened in the light of a ruby sun setting behind the Eerie Mountains on the far shore. Water stretched as far as the eye could see.

"Oh, Bella," said Lila. "What a wonderful view."

"Um, Lila," said Bella. "How do we steer these things? I mean an acorn balloon is all very well but if we're not careful we'll drift out of school."

"No, we won't," said Lila, still staring at the lake. "Hey Bella, isn't that *The Golden Queen* heading our way?"

"The royal barge?" exclaimed Bella. "All the

more reason to get down. It might be the King and Queen coming to visit Bee Balm."

"It's a little late for a royal visit, isn't it?" asked Lila. "But let's find Meggie just in case. She wouldn't want to miss it."

Lila reached over to tap Bella's balloon, and promptly fell off her own. Both balloons popped. Bella screamed with laughter and Lila tried to catch the acorns. They plummeted earthward with Lila fluttering after them.

"Feathers," cried Lila, pointing her wand. With a burst of purple stars the two acorns became as light as swansdown. Now they were easy to catch. Lila turned the floating feathers back into acorns and put them in her pocket.

They flew as fast as they could toward the Star Clan turret and tapped on their bedroom window. Meggie, brushing back her yellow-ocher hair, looked up from her sewing, and hurried to let them in.

A Surprise Visit

"Come quickly," Bella cried. "The royal barge is coming."

The news must have gotten around as a number of chattering fairies were hurrying into the garden, looking toward the gatehouse expectantly. The three friends swooped down to join them and before long a grand assembly had gathered by the Bewitching Pool. Lila's teacher, Mistress Pipit, her orange wings sparkling in the fading light, stood ready next to Fairy Godmother Whimbrel, whose purple gown rippled with a silver sheen. Mistress Hawthorn, the librarian, arrived followed by Mistress Arum, the Charm Three teacher.

"It must be the King and Queen," said Bella. "Otherwise why the great turnout?"

Lila was as excited as her friends, even though she had seen the King and Queen many times before and had even spoken to them. That was one of the advantages of living at the Fairy Palace and working in the royal kitchen, where Cook had taken care of Lila since she was a tiny baby.

The crowd of pupils parted as Princess Bee Balm made her way to the front.

"Ah, there you are, Bee Balm," said Fairy Godmother Whimbrel. "You have a visitor."

"Which will it be?" Meggie asked. "The King or the Queen?"

But it was neither. Through the arch of the gatehouse strode the gaunt, black-robed figure of the Lord Chamberlain. With a cry of delight Princess Bee Balm rushed forward to greet him.

"Your Majesty," said the Lord Chamberlain, taking off his hat and bending his tall figure into a stiff bow. Remembering royal protocol, the Princess stopped her impetuous charge and held out her hand. The Lord Chamberlain pressed her fingers to his lips. "I am on a royal mission, Majesty, and your parents asked me to call in. They wish for your news." From under his cloak he took out a large white letter with a golden seal upon it. "And they requested I deliver this to you as I sailed by." The Princess looked a little disgruntled and her cheeks turned pink. Lila guessed she couldn't have written home for a while. "And, may I also take this opportunity to drop off this little token of my own affection," he added, handing the Princess a pink, gossamer bag threaded with shimmering fairy gold. The Princess, her sparkling best, curtsied.

"Thank you, Lord Chamberlain," she said in her most regal voice. "Most kind." The Lord Chamberlain bowed again and his lips twitched into a crooked smile.

"He's horrible," whispered Bella.

"Shush," said Lila. The Lord Chamberlain's eyes were upon them in an instant. Lila bent her head and curtsied under his hooded gaze.

"Ah, Cook's little kitchen fairy," said the Lord Chamberlain. "I hope you are behaving yourself?" Lila wasn't too sure what to say to that but the

A Surprise Visit

Lord Chamberlain didn't expect a reply and turned away. "A brief word, Headteacher."

Fairy Godmother Whimbrel stepped forward and she and the Lord Chamberlain moved away to exchange a few private words. Then he nodded his head and Fairy Godmother Whimbrel curtsied.

"Well, Headteacher, I must be gone," said the awe-inspiring fairy for all to hear, grandly wrapping his black cloak around himself. "Affairs of state, dear lady, affairs of state." The Lord Chamberlain gave one final haughty bow to the assembled teachers, who returned him deep curtsies. Then, he replaced his hat upon his head and strode away through the gateway without a backward glance, his cloak billowing behind him.

"Lilac Blossom, Harebell, do try and be more respectful in the future," said Fairy Godmother Whimbrel looking across at them over her spectacles. "You do not mutter in the presence of greatness." Then she disappeared leaving a cloud of purple stars popping behind her. With a quick glance in their direction, Mistress Pipit vanished after her. Lila was certain their teacher was trying not to smile.

Gradually, the fairies dispersed, including Bee Balm, tossing her hair and holding the still unopened pink bag tightly. She was surrounded by a simpering group of Sun Clan fairies, eager to know what was inside it. Yet before going into the Hall of Rainbows, she searched the fairy faces in the garden, saw Lila's, and smiled as though it had been Lila she was looking for. Waving, she disappeared indoors.

"Was that wave meant for us?" Bella asked, looking around to see who else it might have been for.

"I don't know," said Lila, feeling uneasy. "But it did seem like it was for us, didn't it?"

"That is the most glorious pink bag I have ever

A Surprise Visit

seen," Meggie exclaimed, now that the Lord Chamberlain's present was lost to view.

Lila fluttered across to the gatehouse and joined several other fairies looking out over the drawbridge to the jetty. Captain Klop, the dragon gatekeeper, was casting off the final mooring rope, the sail was half hoisted and the elf-oarsmen were getting ready to row. *The Golden Queen* was continuing her journey across the Great Silver Lake carrying the Lord Chamberlain away to complete his royal mission. Lila shivered, glad to see him go.

Chapter Three

Assembly

Back in their Star Clan bedroom, Bella bounced onto her bed and turned a somersault. Ignoring Bella's high spirits, Meggie said thoughtfully, "There's something very creepy about the Lord Chamberlain. I can see why you and Cook don't like him very much, Lila."

"Wiggling wellipedes, he's a pompous black insect," said Bella. "And what about that sinister snake wand. Horrible!"

"Did you see it?" Lila asked.

Assembly

"Yes, I caught a glimpse of it under his cloak. Who'd trust a fairy with a wand like that? But Princess Bee Balm really seems to like him. It's amazing!"

"Perhaps it's because he gives her extravagant presents?" said Meggie.

"Funny you should say that," said Lila. "What do you think was in the pink bag?"

"Oh, Lila, wasn't it beautiful," cried Meggie. "Those threads of fairy gold! And woven into the gossamer with such skill. And the pink perfectly matches Bee Balm's hair and frock. I would love to be able to make something like that."

"One day, Meggie, you will," smiled Lila. "Fairies will find out how clever you are and ask you to make bags just like it."

"Do you think so?"

"I know so," said Lila.

"Oh, that reminds me," said Meggie, "I've been reading a really useful book in the library called

Bugs and Butterflies

Fairy Gossamer – Weaves and Colors. I'm going to experiment with making some purple fabric for you, Lila. If I can get the color tone right I'll be able to make you anything you like!"

"Oh, Meggie, you are so thoughtful," said Lila, giving her a hug.

"I was hoping to find a helpful hint on how to make my scissor charm turn into real scissors. It would be useful to have a pair ready at the flick of a wand whenever I need them."

"None of us has managed to make our first day charms do anything magical yet," said Lila, gazing wistfully at the little silver unicorn dangling on her school bracelet. "There are so many other exciting things going on, I keep forgetting to try. But I would like to think that one day I can bring my unicorn to life and go galloping up to the stars on his back. Wow, that would be exciting." And it was a real possibility, Fairy Godmother Whimbrel had once told Lila so.

Assembly

"Mmm," said Bella, giving her little silver charm a passing glance. "To be honest, I've given up with my elfin hat. I can't see any point to it."

There was a knock and Musk Mallow popped her head around the door.

"I knew you wouldn't be ready for bed! The bells are going to ring any minute." Then her crossness evaporated and she broke into a smile. "By the way, well played, you two. Lila, you're a real possibility for the team. Keep her practicing, Bella. I'd like to have you both playing for the Star Clan." And then she was gone.

There were whoops of delight as the three fairies scrambled to get into their nightdresses. Lila placed her wand beside her bed and was snuggling down, feeling really pleased, as the bells rang.

"Well," said Meggie, laughing. "If you both make the Bugs and Butterflies team I will be your biggest fan."

Bugs and Butterflies

"We're trying our hardest, don't you worry," said Lila. The three fairies called out goodnight to one another, closed their eyes and were soon fast asleep.

The following morning Lila was thoroughly enjoying a first long lesson on Plant Power and Potency. She had drawn a beautiful buttercup and was doing a final bit of coloring when Mistress Pipit said, "Quills and coloring pencils down, please." As the school bells rang for break time, Lila's scroll rolled itself up and flew with all the others to her teacher's desk.

"I'm starving," whispered Bella. "I hope we get caraway buns for our snack."

"I don't wish to hear talking, Bella," said Mistress Pipit with one of her stern looks. "After break I would like you to gather by the Bewitching Pool. We're having an assembly. Off you go and get some fresh air. And Bella, you'll be pleased to know there *will* be caraway buns. I have it on the best authority."

They were soon relaxing outside in the garden. Not unexpectedly, Bella finished munching her caraway bun long before Lila and Meggie had finished theirs.

"I think we'll find out something interesting in today's assembly," Bella said, teasingly, as she brushed crumbs from her frock.

"What?" asked Lila.

"Not telling. I want you to have a delightful surprise."

Obviously Bella knew what was going to happen from last year, but Lila knew that no amount of persuading would make her tell them anything if she didn't want to and, by the time the bells rang for the end of break, she and Meggie were none the wiser.

The Charm One fairies gathered by the

Bugs and Butterflies

Bewitching Pool as they had been instructed and Mistress Pipit led the way through the great door of the Hall of Rainbows. They settled themselves in their places while Mistress Pipit seated herself on her throne with the other mistresses on the stage. Princess Bee Balm niftily moved up to sit next to Meggie, one place away from Lila. She smiled at them both. Lila looked at her suspiciously. Bee Balm usually made a point of sitting as far away from her as possible.

"Do you like my new bag, Nutmeg?" the Princess asked Meggie.

"Yes, it's beautiful."

"The Lord Chamberlain always gives such expensive presents," the Princess said. "He loves me very much, you know."

Bella spluttered into her hand and Lila gave her a dig. The Princess looked annoyed. She stroked the bag with her fingertips.

"This is one of his best presents yet," she said

coolly. Then with a sweet smile she turned to whisper something to Sea Holly. Sea Holly giggled and she got a dig from the Princess.

"Flaunting her wealth," whispered Bella. "She just can't help herself." Lila didn't know what the Princess was up to but she didn't think it was anything to do with showing off. It was more than mystifying.

Fairy Godmother Whimbrel arrived and everyone stood up. The Headteacher raised her purple wand and an expectant hush fell.

"Good morning, fairies," she said.

"Good morning, Fairy Godmother Whimbrel," the pupils replied, curtsying then making themselves comfortable again.

"Now the first thing we're going to do at this morning's assembly is the ribbon draw. I know you're very excited about the first Bugs and Butterflies matches of the season. In a few minutes I will reveal which clan is playing against which."

Assembly

Bella grinned.

So that was what the assembly was about. Lila grinned back, her tummy fluttering with excitement. *What was going to happen next?*

"Last year's winners were the Sun Clan..." Cheers broke out from the Sun Clan fairies and Fairy Godmother Whimbrel good-naturedly raised her wand for silence. "And the trophy will remain on display here in the Hall of Rainbows, decorated with its orange ribbon, until this year's champions are decided in the summer."

Lila closed her eyes and imagined the trophy with a silver Star Clan ribbon instead of an orange Sun Clan one. If only, if only!

"And now for the first draw of the year," Fairy Godmother Whimbrel said. With a wave of her wand a flurry of silver, white, yellow and orange ribbons danced above her head: silver for the Star Clan, orange for the Sun Clan, white for the Cloud Clan and yellow for the Moon Clan. With another commanding wave the ribbons paired, tying themselves into two bows, one a mix of silver and orange ribbon, the other a mix of white and yellow.

"The draw is made," smiled Fairy Godmother Whimbrel as the bows shimmered in the air. "The Moons will play the Clouds and the Stars will play the Suns. I wish all the players the very best of luck." There were cheers and a round of applause. Lila couldn't help a glance in Bee Balm's direction. The Princess was cheering as loudly as anyone. Lila smiled ruefully, for now the draw had made them real rivals.

Chapter Four

A Glittering Present

Lila hardly remembered what the rest of the assembly was about. She was busy playing Bugs and Butterflies in her head. It was only when Fairy Godmother Whimbrel dismissed them and they were allowed to talk again that she joined in with the excited chatter.

"It's a shame we have to play the Sun Clan first," said Bella.

"Why? Do you think they'll win?" Lila asked.

"They were such a good team last year. They

Bugs and Butterflies

beat us twice," Bella said.

"And we'll beat you this year," said the Princess, eavesdropping. "The Suns are undoubtedly best. We'll win the trophy again, you wait and see."

"Not necessarily," said Lila, unwilling to be put down. "Just because your clan won last year doesn't automatically mean it'll win this year."

"Oh, yes it does. We'll win, no doubt about it," said Bee Balm, linking arms with Sea Holly and ending the conversation by walking off.

"Pompous pink pest!" Bella shouted after her.

"Don't, Bella," said Lila. "It's not worth it. And anyway, how can Bee Balm possibly know who'll win? She's just being annoying."

"She certainly is," said Meggie.

The three friends went out into the garden and sat by the Bewitching Pool with the sun bright above them, free now until the bells rang for lunch.

A Glittering Present

"The mail's arrived," said Meggie, looking across to the gatehouse where a flock of doves was pulling the mail balloon, its basket of letters suspended underneath. The birds ferried the mail from Silver Spires every morning and took the school mail to town in the afternoon. Captain Klop tossed the birds some well-earned corn.

"Anyone expecting anything?" Meggie asked.

"Not me," said Lila. "Oh no, I don't believe it. Here comes the Princess again."

Bee Balm and Sea Holly were strolling toward them from the other side of the Bewitching Pool. Lila wondered what she wanted this time. Bee Balm's cornflower-blue eyes were glinting with laughter as she approached.

"Have you received your package yet, Lilac Blossom?" she asked.

"What package?"

"Oh, there now, I've spoiled the surprise! There's something in the mail for you. I saw it

Bugs and Butterflies

sticking out from your pigeonhole. Don't forget to pick it up. Come along, Sea Holly."

"When did Bee Balm have time to look? The mail balloon's only just gotten here," Bella said.

"Well, I think it's lovely that she's being nice for a change," said Meggie. "It's kind of relaxing."

"Let's see if there really is a package," said Lila.

They crossed the grass to the gatehouse and curtsied to the old dragon who was sorting letters into the correct pigeonholes on the wall.

"Good morning, Captain Klop," Lila said. "We've come to see if there's anything for us."

"It so happens there is, Lilac Blossom," replied the dragon gruffly. "Here it be." And Captain Klop pulled a small package from the mail basket wrapped up in brown paper and tied up with string. "Says to Lilac Blossom, Charm One Class, Silverlake Fairy School, and there's no other Lilac Blossom than you." He handed the package to Lila.

Bugs and Butterflies

"Thank you, Captain Klop," she said, with a little bob.

"Go on, off you go and open it," said the dragon. "And let me get finished with this sorting. Everyone'll be wanting mail in a minute and the doves were late today."

The three fairies skipped back across the grass and sat by the Bewitching Pool in the shade of the mermaid fountain.

"Bee Balm was right," said Lila, examining the package. "I think it's Cook's writing. I wonder what she's sent me?"

"Go on, don't just sit there looking at it," urged Bella. "Open it."

As soon as Lila took hold of the string there was a little jump on her left wrist and a tingle from her school bracelet.

"Hurry up, Lila. I want to know what's inside!"

"Bella, it's Lila's package," Meggie said.

A Glittering Present

"Patience! Let her open it when she's ready."

"I thought," Lila began, and took hold of the string again. "No, no, it's nothing." She pulled the bow undone. Inside was a letter and something wrapped in rainbow tissue paper. She unfolded the paper carefully and revealed two beautiful purple shoes interwoven with threads of sparkling fairy silver.

"Triple jumping podbugs," said Bella.

Lila stared at the shoes in astonishment.

"Oh, they're beautiful," Meggie gasped, leaning over to get a better look.

"But I never wear shoes and they must have cost a fortune, weeks and weeks of Cook's wages," said Lila. "Why would she suddenly send me shoes?"

Meggie picked up the letter and handed it to her. "Read what she says."

With trembling fingers Lila opened the envelope.

Bugs and Butterflies

"'Dear Lilac Blossom,

*Warmest greetings from us all at the Fairy
Palace kitchen. I know how much you hope to be
selected for the Star Clan's Bugs and Butterflies
team. That being so, I've saved up and bought you
a delightful pair of shoes in your color. Wear them
for luck every time you play. Don't forget!*

With love from your friend,

Cook'."

"Is that all it says?" Bella asked.

Lila stared at the letter. It was such an unusual
one for Cook to write. She only ever called her
Lilac Blossom when she was cross, and for Cook
to call herself Lila's *friend* felt very strange indeed.
She had always signed "With love from Cook"
before. If the letter hadn't been in such familiar
handwriting Lila would have thought it was from
someone else. And why had Cook sent shoes
when she knew Lila preferred bare feet?

"Try them on," said Meggie, stroking the

A Glittering Present

gossamer fabric. "They are spectacularly special."

Lila shook off her misgivings and slipped her foot into one of the shoes. And this time she was certain her unicorn charm jumped. In the past this had meant danger.

"They are very pretty," she agreed, uneasily. "And my size."

"Is that your present?" Bee Balm's voice startled Lila. "Very pretty shoes, don't you think, Sea Holly?" Sea Holly gave a little smirk. "Who are they from?"

"Cook," said Lila.

"Oh, Cook," nodded Bee Balm and there was just something in the way she said it. Lila searched for her meaning but the Princess was not giving anything away. "How kind Cook is," she continued. "Why don't you wear them for the Star Clan selection trial tomorrow? You'll look gorgeous. We're coming to watch, aren't we, Sea Holly?" Her friend smiled obediently. "To size up the competition," Bee Balm added with a laugh. "Come along, Sea Holly. Things to do." And with a swish of her pink gossamer frock, the Princess fluttered away across the grass.

Lila turned helplessly to Meggie.

"But I never wear shoes," she said.

"You must wear them. They're a special present from Cook. And Bee Balm's right, they're gorgeous."

Lila gave Meggie a hug. "It was very kind of Cook, of course it was. And I will write to her right away and thank her."

But secretly, Lila wished she could have remained barefoot. She found the shoes stiff and unwieldy. Perhaps it was the silver thread that made them like that? At least the stiffness wouldn't bother her once she was flying. She would wear the shoes as instructed when she played tomorrow. She carefully rewrapped them in the tissue paper.

A Glittering Present

"I suppose I am a very lucky fairy," Lila said, but then she had a sudden thought. "How did Bee Balm know the package was a present?"

"Packages usually are presents, aren't they?" said Bella.

"The trouble is, Lila, we're far too used to Bee Balm being mean," said Meggie. "When she's nice like this we can't quite believe she means it."

"I suppose so," said Lila. "Anyway, I have a letter to write. I'm going back to the Star turret to do it before the bells ring for lunch. I want to get it in this afternoon's mail."

And she was off at a gallop, running across the grass to the Hall of Rainbows with her package tucked under her arm, imagining she was racing on the back of a handsome unicorn. Meggie and Bella fluttered after her.

Chapter Five

The Team Trial

With her thanks and her news sent to Cook at the palace kitchen, Lila woke the following day more excited than she could ever remember. The lessons part of the day went slowly but, eventually, it was over, and her spirits soared as the Star Clan fairies gathered in the Bugs and Butterflies ring. There was a surprising number of spectators sitting in the surrounding trees, among them Bee Balm and Sea Holly. The Princess was clasping the bag the Lord Chamberlain had given her, with an expression of eager anticipation.

Lila pulled on the beautiful shoes that Cook had sent her. The Princess waved merrily from her comfortable seat and the little silver unicorn jumped. The tingle ran from Lila's bracelet right up her arm. She didn't know what to think. Was the Princess just being friendly, or wasn't she?

"Good luck," Meggie said. "I will cheer you both on like anything." And she gave Lila and Bella a hug before fluttering to a place that Candytuft, another Charm One fairy, had saved for her.

Musk Mallow planted the magical silver sunflower in the center of the ring and the players gathered around to find out what they were going to do. Lila wiggled her toes. In her letter home she had promised Cook she would wear the shoes whenever she played but she was not used to having anything on her feet and the shoes felt very uncomfortable.

Bugs and Butterflies

"Today, as you can see, we're going to practice using real bugs and butterflies," Musk Mallow told them. "You're going to need all your skills as you will be playing against each other. Keep using the defensive somersaults we worked on last time. Remember, you need *eyes in the back of your head*. The fairies who catch the most bugs and butterflies are the fairies I want in my team. Play your best, everyone."

Although Lila didn't much like the idea of playing against Bella, she was certainly going to do just that. Musk Mallow tapped the sunflower with her midnight-blue wand. The silver seeds scattered in a shower across the grass. Flowers, shrubs, grasses and trees grew in the blink of an eye. Soon there was a thick undergrowth of hiding places for bugs, butterflies and fairies alike. A trill of fairy bells rang out and play began.

The first butterfly, a Glistening Blue, fluttered skyward. Several fairies began chasing it. Lila waited behind a little bush. She didn't want to get caught out in a crowd and there would be plenty more butterflies to come. Her feet felt heavy in Cook's shoes but she quickly forgot about that when a wellipede appeared. She ran after it, grinning at the two rows of little booted feet rushing to escape. She stretched out her wand to tap the wellipede's tail...and fell over. By the time she got up the wellipede was gone.

"What happened?" Lila asked herself, feeling stupid. "I should have gotten that one easily." She couldn't see anything that might have tripped her.

A Satin Green butterfly settled on a nearby flower and folded its wings. This time Lila was more careful. But before she could reach it the butterfly took to the air. *Remember, eyes in the back of your head*, Lila told herself. It was just as well. Clover, a nifty flyer, was swooping down behind her. Lila carefully timed her defensive somersault, but turned as though her feet were stuck in mud. It was sheer luck that Bella tapped Clover's shoulder first or Lila would have been out of the game. Instead, it was poor Clover who went out. But even when Lila reached for the butterfly, Bella beat her to it and, with a puff of blue stars, it was gone.

Lila quickly dropped to the ground in case Bella came after her. She couldn't make out why she was being so useless. Then she promptly tripped over a burrowing tufty-tail that disappeared underground before she had a chance to reach for it. She had missed another bug and lost a shoe.

Lila kicked off the other one. Present or not, there was no point in wearing only one shoe. At once, she felt better. Bare feet were best. She had already missed several chances but was determined to make amends. A Darting Red butterfly fluttered earthward, its wings sparkling gloriously. Several other fairies were after it too. Lila raced for the

The Team Trial

butterfly desperate to get there first.

The Darting Red dived steeply. Lila followed, flattening her own wings to her back for speed. It was a brave move and not one she had practiced much, but she badly wanted to score after her dismal start.

The butterfly swerved but not quickly enough. Lila's wand caught it neatly on the tail and it vanished in a puff of purple stars. She had scored one butterfly. She glimpsed a flash of yellow and saw Primrose was chasing her. Instinctively, she somersaulted, executing a perfect turn. Lila tapped poor Primrose on the shoulder and put her out instead. It was good to be playing well at last.

Below her another tufty-tail was running in the grass. It would burrow in an instant if it saw her. She landed cautiously and stopped. Above her an acorn was dangling from a small branch. Or was it a podbug in disguise? She really didn't want to get podded if she could help it. She gave the acorn

a gentle push with her wand. She was right; a podbug leaped at once. If she hadn't ducked she would have been caught by the black and hairy thing. She was delighted to catch the bug instead.

One butterfly and one bug so far. Not too bad a score. And she was lucky, the tufty-tail still hadn't seen her. She pounced, tapping its tail before it had a chance to burrow. Lila was really on a roll now. Three more bugs disappeared in a pop of purple stars after which she caught another six butterflies, ending up with a score of twelve by the time the bells rang for the end of play.

Lila dropped to the ground breathless but pleased, glad to see Bella was still in the game.

"Well done, Lila," said Bella. "Nobody got you out."

"No, but I was terrible at the start," she replied, still annoyed with herself for that. "I scored twelve. What did you get?"

"Eighteen," said Bella. Lila's heart sank. That

was six more than her score. All she could do was hope that twelve would be enough to get her on the team.

The Star fairies gathered around Musk Mallow for the verdict and Meggie flew down to join them.

"What happened to you at the beginning?" Meggie asked Lila. "And where are your new shoes?"

"My shoes!" cried Lila. In the heat of the game she had forgotten all about them. There they were, lying on the grass and she fluttered over to pick them up. She didn't put them on but glanced up to where Bee Balm and Sea Holly had been sitting, but they had already gone.

"Well done, everyone," said Musk Mallow, as Lila fluttered back. "There was some excellent play and some very good scores." Musk Mallow held a scroll in her hand and she began to read from it. "The team for our first match starts with

The Team Trial

Linnet and Harebell who both scored eighteen." Bella's face split into a big grin. "Next come Saffron, Foxglove and Violet, each with a score of sixteen, then Cornflower, with fifteen." Lila held her breath. The Stars needed one more player. *Please, please let it be me.* "And finally Rose with thirteen."

Lila could hardly believe it. She had missed out by one point. She smiled bravely.

"Well done, Bella," she said. "You and Linnet had the best score."

"Shush a minute, I haven't finished," said Musk Mallow. "Our first reserve is you, Lilac Blossom, with twelve. You played well once you got going."

First reserve, Lila thought and, to her dismay, she felt tears pricking her eyes. *I am not going to cry*, she told herself. *I can't play and that's that. I will watch the game and enjoy it. To be first reserve will have to be good enough.* But something was nagging at her, and she couldn't put a finger

Bugs and Butterflies

on what it was, because one thought overrode everything else; if she had caught the two bugs and the butterfly she had missed at the beginning of the game she would definitely have been on the team.

Chapter Six

Shoe Mystery

When Musk Mallow had gone Meggie slipped her arm through Lila's. Lila barely noticed, she was so deep in thought, and continued tapping the purple shoes against her leg. Then she squeezed Meggie's arm in an absent-minded sort of way. She simply couldn't forgive herself for playing so badly at the start of the trial.

"Have you still got the acorns?" Bella asked. "We could have an acorn balloon ride."

"But don't you want to stay and watch the Sun

Bugs and Butterflies

Clan trial?" Meggie said. "They're next in the Bugs and Butterflies ring."

"Not one bit," said Lila, feeling in her pocket for the acorns.

"Hey, but that's a good point! We ought to be sizing up the opposition," said Bella. "And rumor has it that Bee Balm is playing incredibly well, which I find hard to believe."

"Look, why don't you two stay?" Lila said. "Right now, watching Bee Balm play well is the last thing I want to do. If she gets onto the Sun Clan team I will just pop with jealousy."

"Yes, yes, sorry, silly idea," said Bella. "What am I thinking? Acorn balloons are much more fun."

"What are you going to do, Meggie?" Lila asked.

"Come with you, of course," Meggie smiled.

Lila held out her hand with the three acorns in it. "Get ready to fly." She lightly touched each acorn with her wand. "Acorn balloons," she commanded. The acorns quickly puffed up, and as soon as they were big enough, Bella dived onto one and took hold of the stalk.

"Come on, Meggie," she cried. "It's really comfy lying like this."

Meggie copied Bella and Lila flopped onto the remaining balloon. The three fairies drifted silently skyward.

"It's so peaceful," Meggie said. "No whooshing of wings or wind in your ears."

"That's right, and it's very relaxing," said Lila. "Acorn balloons are one of my better ideas." She turned onto her back and looked up at the sky, rolling the little unicorn charm between her fingers and thinking of how he always warned her of danger. She suddenly flipped over again and looked down at the Bugs and Butterflies ring. The trial had begun and fairies were madly chasing each other in and out of the foliage. Lots of fairies were watching and so was Captain Klop.

Shoe Mystery

Somewhere among them were Princess Bee Balm and Sea Holly. Had the unicorn jumped earlier because the Princess was nearby and she meant danger? Or was there some other reason and, if so, what else might be dangerous? She needed to find out.

"I've changed my mind," Lila called. "I do want to watch some of the Sun Clan match."

"Okay," said Bella. "If we drop down a little we'll easily make out everyone."

"All right with you, Meggie?" Lila asked, guiding the balloons with her wand.

"Of course," said Meggie. "It's a fantastic view from up here."

"There's Bee Balm," said Bella, sharp eyed as ever. "By that bush near the center of the ring."

Bee Balm ducked under a branch and quickly leaped to catch a wellipede. Then she whizzed into the air after a Darting Red, the hardest type of butterfly to catch, as it lived up to its name. But

Bugs and Butterflies

the Princess caught it easily before somersaulting around an opposing team member and catching her as well. Lila was astonished.

"Podbugs alive," gasped Bella. "If that isn't fantastic play, I don't know what is? Oh dear, and poor old Sea Holly's out already."

"The Princess is wearing new shoes," said Meggie. "I can tell by the gold thread. It's the same fabric as the gorgeous gossamer bag."

"Butterburs and bodkins, I wonder if..." said Lila. "Hold tight to your stalks, everybody." And with a skilful flick of her wand the acorn balloons were off, flying as if they were speedy airships.

"Super-stardust-fantastic," cried Bella as they zoomed toward the Star Clan turret and, one after the other, flew in through their bedroom window.

"What did you do that for?" cried Meggie, giggling. "I nearly fell off."

Lila turned the balloons back into acorns and flung Cook's shoes on the floor.

Shoe Mystery

"Oh, Lila, no, how could you?" cried Meggie, rushing to pick them up.

"I may have a good reason," said Lila. "Remember how badly I played at the start of our practice? Once I stopped wearing the new shoes I was fine. Now *I* think that's odd."

"Are you saying there's something wrong with the shoes?" Meggie asked, carefully looking them over. "They look all right to me."

"Let me get this straight," said Lila, pacing the room. "I tripped over the burrowing tufty-tail and that's when the first shoe came off. I got rid of the other one and then, yes, I chased the Darting Red and caught it easily. It was after I got rid of them that my playing improved."

Meggie put the shoes back on the floor. "Yes, I see what you mean," she said, looking at them suspiciously. "But how can you be sure it's something to do with the shoes? It might be because you don't normally wear them."

Bugs and Butterflies

"Oh come on, Meggie, everything else was the same as before, my wand, my frock. You can't expect me to believe that shoes would make that much of a difference?" Lila said. "But they *did*."

"It does make sense," said Bella.

"But *Cook* sent you the shoes," said Meggie. "It doesn't make sense to *me*."

"And look at Bee Balm, superb flying, perfect somersaults. How come she's suddenly so great? She's been a very average player until very recently," Lila continued. "From the day the Lord Chamberlain arrived."

"That's true," said Bella, listening attentively.

"And what's she wearing? Shoes! Shoes made of the same fabric as the bag he gave her. I think Bee Balm's amazing play has something to do with him."

"That might be jumping to conclusions," said Meggie. "We don't even know for sure there were shoes in the bag."

Shoe Mystery

"It doesn't feel like jumping to conclusions to me," said Lila, pacing the room. "It feels like following clues." Bella slipped the purple shoes onto her feet.

"What are you doing?" Meggie asked as Bella fluttered to the ceiling.

"Trying to decide if Lila's got a point," said Bella and she rolled forward into a clumsy somersault and crashed onto her knees.

"Bella, are you all right!" cried Lila, hurrying to help her up.

"That is totally weird. I've got to try that again to make sure."

"No, don't," said Lila. "You might hurt yourself."

But Bella was already in the air. This time she landed on her feet with a wobble. Bella pulled off the shoes and tossed them to the floor in disgust.

"Normally, I can turn two somersaults from the ceiling. You watch." And she turned one and two and landed neatly with a bounce on her toes. "There's no way I can do that in those shoes. I think Lila's right, they're charmed."

"Exactly," said Lila. "To make me play badly."

"But why would Cook make you play badly?" said Meggie. "It's the last thing she'd want."

"That's the point, Meggie. They're not from Cook. They're from somebody else, somebody who wants me to play badly."

"There's only one person we know who'd want you to do that," Bella said. "Bee Balm! And they can't have been from her because they came in the mail."

"I know," said Lila.

"But wait a minute," said Bella. "I think she knew about them. Lila, don't you remember, Bee Balm told you a package was in your pigeonhole but when Captain Klop handed it to you, he took it from the mail basket?"

Meggie clapped her hand to her mouth.

Shoe Mystery

"She did tell you that. I remember."

"But there's no way that Bee Balm could have sent the shoes from the palace. Somebody else must have sent them for her," said Lila. The three fairies turned to one another with open mouths. "It has to be…" Lila started.

"…the Lord Chamberlain!" Bella finished for her. "Bee Balm could easily have asked him to send charmed shoes pretending they were from Cook. We know he spoils the Princess rotten and we saw him give her a present which must have been her new shoes."

Lila sat crossly on her bed. "Well, if it was a plot hatched by Bee Balm and the Lord Chamberlain, it's worked. They've made sure I won't play for the Star Clan team."

"Oh, Lila, that's terrible," said Meggie, rushing to comfort her.

"And it's true, the Lord Chamberlain is clever. He could easily copy Cook's writing. I thought the letter was worded strangely. 'Dear Lilac Blossom' and 'From your friend, Cook'. Cook always writes 'Dear Lila' and sometimes, 'Dearest Lila' when she's really missing me. Oh, everything's making sense now, Bee Balm being all smiles and interested in the package." Lila jumped up and started pacing again. "And I don't know what to do about it."

"We can steal the Princess's shoes," said Bella. "Hers must be charmed to make her play well. Think how silly she'll look if she can't wear them. After all, she's messed up your chances of a place on the team, that only seems fair."

"No, Bella, we can't," said Lila. "It won't change anything about me being reserve. We must wait for a reply from Cook. Until I have actual proof my shoes weren't from her I can't say anything. What we need is a clever plan to expose what Bee Balm's done. The only trouble is, I can't think of one."

Chapter Seven

Fairy Dance

The news was all around the school the following morning – Princess Bee Balm had been chosen to play for the Sun Clan. She had excelled herself in the trial by performing even better than Marigold, one of the very best players in the whole school. She had amazed every fairy watching. When they met in class Bee Balm was smiling broadly.

"Oh, Lilac Blossom," she said. "What bad luck not making the Star Clan team. I know how hard you tried. You must be *so* disappointed. I would be if I hadn't made it onto the Sun Clan team. It's the same for Sea Holly. She's quite depressed at not being one of us."

Sea Holly frowned. Lila didn't blame her for the black look. Bee Balm couldn't help crowing, and appeared unaware of hurting her friend's feelings.

"Lila's our first reserve," said Bella.

"Yes, but she won't get to play, that's what I mean," said Bee Balm. "Unlike me."

"Well, at least Bella's on the Star Clan team again," said Lila.

"So I hear," said Bee Balm sniffily and then, as Mistress Pipit came toward them, added with a beaming smile. "Well done, Harebell, for getting chosen." Then lowering her voice to almost a whisper she added, "We'll beat you, naturally." And laughing as though she had told a wonderful joke she dragged Sea Holly away.

Fairy Dance

"Well, it looks as if Bee Balm's achieved her ambition," said Lila. "Poor old Sea Holly, I don't know how she stands it."

"Underneath all the pretend friendliness she was just the same old Bee Balm," said Bella.

"It looks that way," agreed Meggie.

The day of the Bugs and Butterflies match dawned and, so far, Lila had failed to come up with a single idea to stop Bee Balm from being on her team. If the Princess continued to play as fantastically the Sun Clan was certain to win the Bugs and Butterflies match. Lila was miserable at the thought of the Stars losing because Bee Balm had cheated. But, unlike her, Bella woke up in a good mood.

"Hey," she said as she sat up in bed. "I've got an idea that might trick Bee Balm into showing what she's been up to. It means wearing the purple shoes one more time, Lila. But if it works it'll be worth it."

"Oh, tell us," said Lila, cheering up at once. She would do anything to stop the Princess if she could.

"It's really very simple," said Bella. "When we go to the Flutter Tower for our dance class, Pipity always leads us in through the roof, doesn't she?"

"Almost always," corrected Meggie.

"I will set up a somersaulting competition," Bella continued, ignoring Meggie. "You start out wearing the purple shoes, Lila. And you know how Bee Balm is always desperate to win, so, if you're wearing the bogus shoes, she'll expect to win. But, as we know, you are a million times better at somersaulting than she is, or at least you were before the charmed shoes, if you see what I mean. So just before we start, we say, 'Shoes off, everyone' and, if Bee Balm refuses, well, we'll know her shoes are charmed."

Fairy Dance

"But how does that help?" Meggie asked. "We already know the shoes are charmed."

"And what happens if she does take them off?" Lila added.

"She'll lose," said Bella. "So she won't, will she?" There was a pause. "Well, all right, so it's not the best idea but at least she'll know we're on to her." Neither Lila nor Meggie said anything. "Okay, does anyone have a better idea?"

"I suppose we could give it a try," said Lila. "I just wish Cook would hurry up and write back."

Later on that morning Lila, Bella and Meggie gathered at the edge of the Wishing Wood on their way to their dance lesson. The rest of the class was already skimming over the trees toward the Flutter Tower where the lesson was going to take place. The three friends had chosen not to fly but to take the path. Just before they came into the clearing by the tower, Lila put on the shoes that Cook was supposed to have given her. She wasn't certain Bella's idea was going to prove anything but it made her feel that at least she was doing something.

"Are you ready, Lila?" Bella asked. "Just leave everything to me." The three friends joined the waiting class.

The Flutter Tower's silver wall shimmered in the morning sun, aided by Captain Klop, who was doing some polishing with a large pink duster. His sharp dragon eyes were watching the fairies and he gave Lila a nod. She bobbed a curtsy in return.

"Hey, everyone," said Bella. "I've just had a fantastic idea. How about a clan somersault competition on the way in? From the top of the Flutter Tower to the bottom? Anyone want to go for the Cloud Clan?"

"I will," volunteered Snowdrop.

"Me for the Moon Clan," said Larkspur.

"Lila, why don't you go for the Star Clan?" said Bella.

Fairy Dance

Bee Balm's eyes darted to Lila's feet. "I'll go for the Sun Clan," the Princess said with a broad smile.

"Okay then, it's Snowdrop, Larkspur, Lila and Bee Balm somersaulting for the glory of their clans. When Pipity leads us in, I'll say 'go'."

"Very well, Harebell," said Bee Balm, brimming with confidence. Bella winked at Lila. Bee Balm, pointing her toes in her pink and golden shoes, was limbering up. "I think you'll find I'll win," she said.

They didn't have to wait long. Mistress Pipit arrived beside them in a spray of orange suns.

"Ready?" said Bella.

"No shoes," said Lila, taking hers off and tossing them to Bella.

"I'm keeping mine on," said Bee Balm quickly.

"Why?"

"Because I want to."

"Okay," said Bella, glancing at Lila. But then all their plans were dashed when Mistress Pipit pointed her wand at the Flutter Tower and a door appeared and opened. They weren't going in by the roof entrance after all. There was a general air of disappointment at the loss of the competition and Bella looked particularly fed up as her plan to expose Bee Balm had failed.

"Fairies, please find a safe place for your wands," Mistress Pipit said, leading them inside. "And I want everyone barefoot, please."

As the fairies skipped to put down their wands, and those who were wearing them, to take off their shoes, Bee Balm sulkily slipped off hers and put them in the gossamer bag, which she left near the door. Bella plonked down the offending purple shoes close by. The door closed, shutting out the birdsong from the Wishing Wood, but a slip of pink duster was caught in the hinge, which stopped the door from vanishing as it usually did. Lila wrinkled her nose. *Poor Captain Klop. How was he going to get his duster free?*

"Gather round, please," said Mistress Pipit.

Fairy Dance

"Today we're going to go over some of the fairy dances we've learned this autumn. I'm going to play several different pieces of music and I want to see if you can remember which dance goes with which tune. I'll give you a clue to the first dance. It shares my name."

"Dance of the Meadow Pipit," whispered Lila. Bella and Meggie nodded. This was a dance that began slowly and ended with lots of twirls and spins.

"Ready, everybody? And I want to see those toes pointing."

The orange sun at the tip of Mistress Pipit's wand glowed brightly and the music began. Lila spread her arms wide and fluttered gently into the air. The music chirruped and fluted. Lila joined hands with the other Star Clan fairies, Meggie, Bella, Cowslip, Periwinkle and Primrose. It was as if the Flutter Tower was full of meadow pipits singing their little hearts out. It was impossible not to enjoy such a dance. Around they went, a whirl of yellows, blues and purple, breaking apart to end with the fastest twirl they could manage.

The next tune was the Dance of the Ladybug. Lila entwined fingers with Meggie and Periwinkle and the fairies weaved arches and spun in gentle circles until the music changed again.

"It's the Daffodil Dance this time," said Lila. The fairies took up the bobbing and swaying rhythm. They tossed their heads, kept their toes pointing and stretched their arms to the ends of their fingertips. Again the music changed, this time the melody was gentle and slow.

"Oh, I've forgotten this one," said Meggie.

"It's the Dance of the Willow Tree," Lila and Cowslip said together. The Star Clan fairies fluttered and swayed in a little group imitating slender willow branches rippling in a breeze.

"Oh, yes, how could I have forgotten it?" cried Meggie.

Bugs and Butterflies

When the last of the music faded away the fairies landed breathless on the floor.

"What elegant dancers I have in my class," smiled Mistress Pipit as her pupils clustered around her, their faces glowing. "Graceful, rhythmic and all of you caught the mood of the music beautifully. Well done. Now, when you've gotten your breath back, we'll finish with whichever dance you choose."

Everyone wanted to repeat the Dance of the Meadow Pipit. It left Lila surprised to find she was happy in spite of all her cares. *Dancing gives me such a lovely feeling*, she thought, and went to pick up her wand. She noticed that the pink duster had disappeared. Somehow Captain Klop had gotten it back again and the door had vanished into the wall as it usually did.

"My shoes! Where are my shoes? I've got the bag but my shoes are gone." Bee Balm's voice rose in a fury. "Somebody's taken my shoes!"

Fairy Dance

Everyone stopped what they were doing. "There's a thief in the school." Bee Balm turned on Lila. "It was you, wasn't it?"

"Of course it wasn't me. How could it possibly have been me? I've been dancing all the time," said Lila, stung by the accusation. She had no idea where the shoes were and was just as puzzled as everyone else. But there was one other odd thing; Lila's shoes were also missing.

"That's enough, Bee Balm," said Mistress Pipit. "Wild hysteria does not help find a pair of mislaid shoes."

Lila wondered at first if Bella had taken them but she could see that her friend was as mystified as she was. How extraordinary! None of the other fairies wearing shoes had lost them. Now what was Bee Balm going to do? She was due to play in the clan match at the end of the afternoon and, if she didn't find her shoes, how good a player would she be without them?

Chapter Eight

The Bugs and Butterflies Match

Bee Balm immediately offered a reward – a silver necklace – to anyone who found her missing shoes. While the whole school searched she stood in the Hall of Rainbows and railed against the thief who had stolen them. Lila, Bella and Meggie remained as mystified over their disappearance as the Princess.

"Who could have taken two pairs of shoes from practically under our noses?" said Lila as they sat, mulling over the problem, by the Bewitching Pool.

No sooner were the words said than she felt a tap on her shoulder and turned to find Captain Klop's worn dragon face looking down at her.

"Lilac Blossom, find the Princess," he said with a firm and steady voice. "Bring her to the gatehouse. Tell her it's urgent. She's to come at once."

"The Princess?"

"Aye, the Princess!"

Lila raced off as fast as she could with Bella and Meggie hurrying behind her. What could Captain Klop possibly want with the Princess? She found Bee Balm, in the Hall of Rainbows, still directing the search.

"Bee Balm!" called Lila, pressing through the throng of fairies fluttering hither and thither. "Bee Balm!"

"What?" snapped the Princess. "Can't you see I'm busy?"

Bugs and Butterflies

"Captain Klop wants you to come to the gatehouse."

"Captain Klop! If he wishes to speak to me, tell him to come here. I will not be ordered about by a dragon."

"He said it's urgent and to come at once."

The Princess's expression underwent a change as she realized why the dragon might want to see her. Lila didn't get a chance to say anything else. Bee Balm pushed her way through the crowd and ran to the door.

"Come on, what are you waiting for?" she yelled at Lila. "He may have found my shoes and I'm not going near that scaly creature on my own."

The dragon was waiting at the gatehouse by his front door. When he saw the fairies coming he indicated they were to follow him and led the way indoors, up some stairs, to a round room with a large stone fireplace. Sitting in the grate were two

The Bugs and Butterflies Match

pairs of shoes; one, a purple pair, that sparkled with silver thread and the other, a pink pair, that shone with fairy gold.

"My shoes!" cried Bee Balm, rushing to claim them. A strong dragon arm barred her way. "Let me have them," she raged.

"Stand still and listen to me," Captain Klop ordered and, seeing it was impossible to push him out of the way, Bee Balm did as she was told. The dragon grunted his approval.

"That's better," he said. "Now listen carefully, Highness. I've asked you here to solve a dilemma I have. In my grate are two pairs of shoes and I'm going to give you a choice. I either burns them within the next few minutes or I takes them to Fairy Godmother Whimbrel and explains what I knows."

"You don't know anything," said Bee Balm.

"I think I do. I have eyes in my head, Majesty. I know that Lilac Blossom's purple shoes make her

The Bugs and Butterflies Match

fly like a clumsy clown and your pink pair turned you into an acrobatic fairy the like of which this school has never seen. Such a sudden and an astonishing improvement in a fairy's abilities, I finds a little suspicious."

"Suspicious! What nonsense," laughed the Princess, but Lila could see that her thoughts were racing. "You can't make accusations like that without proof."

"I have some of the proof I need in this communication," said the dragon, lifting a letter from the table. "I'll read it to you:

'*Dear Captain Klop*', it says here,

'*Your welcome words have explained everything. I could make no sense of Lila's letter thanking me for a pair of new shoes. I SENT HER NONE. It pains my heart to think that my dear one may have been tricked. Please, take whatever action you think necessary to put things right. I am gladder than I can tell to know that you are looking out for her.*

My thanks, as ever,
Cook'."

Captain Klop put the letter down and waited. Lila could not mistake such words; they were obviously written by her beloved Cook. The Princess, her cheeks a stinging pink, was wringing her hands. The dragon got impatient.

"Very well, I'll take the shoes to Fairy Godmother Whimbrel," he said, stepping toward the fireplace.

"No, no, don't do that," said the Princess, laying her wand on his arm. "How am I supposed to know who sent the purple shoes?"

"Well, we know who gave you your shoes, everyone saw him do it," said the dragon.

"No, you didn't, he gave me a little bag. This little bag," said Bee Balm holding it up.

"Identical fabric to the shoes and a perfect size for carrying them. I suggest to you that the person who gave you that bag with shoes inside it was the same person who sent shoes to Lilac Blossom."

"Are you accusing the Lord Chamberlain of doing something underhand?" exclaimed Bee Balm, in her haughty voice.

"I wouldn't dream of doing so," said Captain Klop. "As I said, I merely make a suggestion. Now come on, make up your mind, Majesty. I either takes 'em or I burns 'em. What's it to be?"

"Will I be expelled if anybody finds out?"

"That's what I'm thinking might happen," said the dragon. "Fairy Godmother Whimbrel is not going to take kindly to this sort of trickery."

"This is your fault, Lilac Blossom," said Bee Balm, turning angrily on Lila.

"'Tis nothing to do with Cook's little fairy," snapped the dragon. "You leave her alone. This is all your doing. Ever since the Lord Chamberlain visited I've had my eye on you. Charmed shoes indeed."

Bugs and Butterflies

"But they were his present to me," said Bee Balm, lamely.

"Come on, make up your mind."

Princess Bee Balm closed her eyes. "Very well, burn them, both pairs." And without another word she turned and stalked back down the stairs.

The dragon took a deep breath and blew out a tongue of orange flame. The pink shoes shriveled into black ash. The second flame turned the purple pair to cinders. For a moment Lila and the dragon stared at the smoldering embers.

"Thank you, Captain Klop," said Lila. "Cook's right, you've done me a real kindness."

"Beware of the Lord Chamberlain," said the dragon. "He's your real enemy."

"But why?" asked Lila. "I'm only a kitchen fairy."

"I know," nodded the dragon. "But there's more to the Lord Chamberlain than meets the eye. He schemes, that one, and I don't want to see you getting caught up in his intrigues." He patted Lila's arm. "Shame about you not playing on your team. That Princess is a proper little madam, but I'm keeping an eye out for you. I always will, little Lilac Blossom."

"Thank you, Captain Klop," said Lila. "Thank you very, very much."

"It's what friends is for," said the dragon, kindly. He handed Lila a letter from the table and led her to the top of the stairs. "One for you from Cook. Take care now."

As Lila skipped downstairs she felt all her worries fall away.

Bella and Meggie were waiting for her outside.

"What's happened? Bee Balm's told everyone to stop searching," said Bella. "She's got a face like thunder."

Lila quickly told the story and both fairies listened wide-eyed.

Bugs and Butterflies

"Captain Klop's a hero," said Meggie, when Lila had finished.

"And," added Lila, "I've got a real letter from Cook."

"Open it at once," said Bella. "Darting Reds alive, Bee Balm's really been caught this time."

Laughing, Lila began to read.

"*'Dearest Lila,'*"

"Now that sounds more like Cook," said Meggie.

"*'I did not send you shoes. Nor would I, as I know you prefer to be barefoot. I am sure that by the time you read this letter Captain Klop will have sorted everything out. Always trust the Captain.*

I've not told you this part of your story before, but he was the sea voyager who rescued you from the Ocean of Diamond Waters when you were a little baby, a'floating in the basket.

The Bugs and Butterflies Match

He's grown mighty fond of you as do all that know you. Write to me the outcome of this wickedness. I must have news soon. I'm all of a worry.

Your ever-loving,

Cook

PS I'm all of a fluster too. Almost forgot, Mip sends his love. It was all I could do to stop him from coming to help you.'"

"Oh, Lila," said Meggie. "If only Mip had come."

"What a brave elf!" said Bella. "We've got to meet him. He really wanted to help you!"

"I couldn't wish for a better friend," said Lila. "And you'll both love him. I hope you can meet him soon." She looked down again at the letter. "I'm really glad Cook's told me it was Captain Klop who rescued me when I was a little tiny baby. Just think, if it wasn't for him I might not be here now."

Bugs and Butterflies

The bells rang for lunch. Lila folded up the letter and the three fairies made their way to the refectory trying to decide what other adventures Captain Klop might have had while he was skippering his ship across the great oceans. Then, with her food in front of her, Lila discovered she was really hungry and ate a hearty lunch. They were scraping their dishes after a particularly splendid hazelnut and honey crunch with marigold custard, when Musk Mallow came hurrying in.

"Lilac Blossom, prepare to play," she said. "Linnet has torn a wing and sprained her wrist. You're going to have to take her place in this afternoon's match."

"But Linnet's one of our best players," said Lila.

"I know," said Musk Mallow. "Do your best. I know you will."

Lila was at once thrilled and appalled. She was going to play on the Star Clan team, the thing she had dreamed about and wished for, but she was to take the place of the player who was second only to Musk Mallow in skill.

"You'll do it," said Bella, giving her a hug. "No longer a reserve; now a true Star Clan player."

At the far end of the table, Sea Holly whispered something in Bee Balm's ear. The Princess scowled, got up, and, swishing her frock in a couldn't-care-less way, left the refectory with her friend chasing after her.

"I think Bee Balm's heard the news," grinned Bella, watching the Princess go.

Lila was glad she'd been told it after she'd finished eating. Her nerves were already kicking in. It was all very well being a reserve, she realized, but when the time came for the reserve to play, a lot rested on her performance.

Afternoon lessons passed in a daze and Mistress Pipit decided to let the players go early.

"I'm sure everyone wishes Bee Balm, Lilac

Bugs and Butterflies

Blossom and Harebell the best of luck for the match this afternoon. I'm delighted that we have three First Years playing."

The class give them a round of applause and Mistress Pipit sent them on their way with a smile. At the top of the Swallow staircase Lila caught up with the Princess.

"Good luck, Bee Balm," she said.

"Oh, very funny, dragon lover. How could you let him burn those beautiful shoes?"

"But you were cheating," said Bella. "And you still don't get it. Cheating is bad. B-A-D. Bad!"

"Oh, go rot your wings," said the Princess and she stomped off down the stairs ahead of them.

"This could be rather embarrassing for her," pondered Lila. "I don't suppose she has any idea how well she'll play without the shoes."

"Don't you dare feel sorry for her, Lila," said Bella. "She'd never feel sorry for you in a million years."

The Bugs and Butterflies Match

"No, I suppose not," said Lila, recognizing the truth in Bella's words.

Musk Mallow assembled her team at the edge of the Bugs and Butterflies ring. Linnet was there too. Her torn wing was neatly stitched and her arm was in a sling.

"Lilac Blossom, I wanted to say good luck," she said, coming over. "You're a good player. You'll do well."

Lila smiled up at the taller fairy.

"I'm sorry you're hurt."

"Just bad luck," Linnet said with a shrug. Then she flew rather raggedly to an oak branch to watch the match from there.

The Sun Clan fairies were gathering around Marigold on the far side of the ring, Bee Balm among them. Marigold was another great player, scarily good. Lila was feeling more nervous than she could ever remember.

"Our first inter-clan match of the year," said

Bugs and Butterflies

Musk Mallow, with a purposeful smile. "You know the tactics. Use them! And if you see any of our team in trouble, help them rather than score. The more of us that stay in the game the better. May the best team win. *Go, go, go, the Stars are mighty*."

The team picked up Musk Mallow's cry and chanted loudly, "*Go, go, go, the Stars are mighty*."

From the far side of the ring Marigold led her team in their rallying cry. "*We are the rising Suns, fierce and fiery. We are the rising Suns, fierce and fiery*." Then the spectators picked up the chants as well.

Mistress Arum, the Charm Three class teacher, and a member of the Moon Clan, arrived to referee the game. She placed the silver sunflower in the center of the ring. The team captains signaled they were ready. Mistress Arum tapped the stalk and the sunflower seeds scattered. Plants, shrubs and trees quickly sprouted. Lila had

The Bugs and Butterflies Match

already seen a wellipede peeking out from under a leaf. She braced herself, ready to fly. The bells for the start of the game rang out.

"*Go, go, go the Stars*," cried Musk Mallow, leading her team in flight. They followed her with a cheer. From the other side of the ring Marigold did the same. The spectators chanted even louder, Meggie among them. The game had begun and Lila and Bella flew into the thick of it.

Chapter Nine

Winners and Losers

At first, Lila ducked and weaved, determined not to be caught by a Sun Clan player right at the start of the game. She wanted to have a good score before that happened. But she soon got into the swing of it and quickly caught two Satin Green butterflies and a Glistening Blue before a trembling leaf caught her eye below. Lila dropped to the ground, certain there was a bug underneath it. She peered carefully between the foliage and saw a wellipede

Winners and Losers

pulling on a boot. But the wellipede saw Lila and scuttled away as fast as its one hundred legs would allow.

She sped after it but remembered; *eyes in the back of your head*. Above her, Marigold was diving toward her. There was no possibility of somersaulting. Lila was on the ground. She did the next best thing; pretended she hadn't seen. Marigold had the narrowest miss, when at the last second, Lila ducked under a leaf. Swinging around the stem, she shot out again and tapped Marigold on the shoulder.

Marigold and Lila stared at one another in disbelief. Then, with a disappointed shrug, Marigold flew out of the ring. Lila could hardly believe it. She had gotten the Sun Clan captain out. The wellipede was long gone and Lila couldn't see anything else to catch among the grasses. She flew into the air to find a battle raging. Fairies were engaged in frantic chases and, in

Bugs and Butterflies

between, butterflies were flitting every which way.

Lila flew low, eyes darting this way and that. Bella was creeping up on a Glistening Blue, resting on a giant red poppy. Stalking her were Bee Balm and a Charm Three fairy called Dropwort. Why hadn't Bella seen them?

"Behind you, Bella," Lila shouted, but in vain: Bella was concentrating on the butterfly. Lila looked over her own shoulder and flew skyward fast to avoid pursuit.

Bee Balm and Dropwort dived to get Bella out.

"Mine," shouted Dropwort, but the Princess ignored her and kept going. With the niftiest flip Lila had ever seen, Bella disappeared underneath them, caught her butterfly and was off. Bee Balm and Dropwort collided with a horrible clash of wands.

"You idiot," said Bee Balm.

"You're the idiot," roared Dropwort indignantly.

Winners and Losers

"That was selfish play. I was closer." And she flew off.

Bee Balm swung around, glaring. But Lila didn't wait to see what she would do next. Bella was beckoning to her from underneath the poppy and Lila dived to join her.

"Lila, you got Marigold out. That's amazing," said Bella.

"How did you know?"

"I saw you do it. You were a whirling wonder."

"*You've* just done the best somersault I've ever seen," said Lila. "Hey, look, two Darting Reds."

"One each," said Bella and the two fairies shot after them. They weren't the only ones. Ahead of them were two Sun Clan fairies. What an opportunity. Bella pointed to the fairy she was going for. Lila grinned and chased the other.

She glanced over her shoulder but there was no one there, so she raced after her opponent,

Bugs and Butterflies

a Charm Four fairy called Lobelia, who had almost reached the Darting Red. Lila stretched forward but, before her wand could make contact, Lobelia somersaulted. Lila lurched sideways, following her wand, in her own defensive loop. Lobelia looked around, surprised, when Lila wasn't where she expected her to be. She was even more surprised when Lila tapped her on the shoulder.

Lobelia was out and Lila, victorious, chased and caught the Darting Red, pleased to see it disappear in a purple puff. She quickly somersaulted just in case but she was still alone. There didn't appear to be as many Sun fairies still flying, as there were Stars.

But the game wasn't over yet. Just below Lila was a bush and her sharp eyes saw it shiver and sway. She plummeted, eager to find out what kind of bug was hiding underneath. A foot slid out and was quickly withdrawn again. Lila came to a fluttering stop. It wasn't a wellipede foot; it was a fairy foot. She crept behind the plant and, gently moving a leaf, saw Bee Balm peeking out in the other direction.

The Princess didn't look as though she was stalking a bug or doing anything very much. And when a burrowing tufty-tail emerged close by, instead of catching it, Bee Balm slunk further under the bush.

"Butterburs and bodkins," Lila whispered under her breath, "she's hiding." Lila gently touched the Princess's shoulder with her wand. Bee Balm yelped and shivered, relaxing when she saw it was Lila and not a bug.

"Okay, I'm out!" she said, and, with a furtive peek, no doubt checking for more bugs, she left her shelter and flew skyward.

Bella dropped down beside Lila.

"Did you get her out?"

Lila nodded and put a finger to her lips.

Bugs and Butterflies

"Somewhere around here is a tufty-tail," she whispered.

The two fairies waited, hardly daring to breathe, and, to their delight, the bug popped its nose out, looked both ways and wiggled across the grass. Bella leaped forward and tapped its tail. At the same time something black and furry dropped onto Bella's head. She was well and truly podded. Lila hurriedly caught the podbug and then helped Bella out.

"Horrible hairy bug," Bella said, giving herself a brush down. "Lucky you were there, Lila. I hate being gotten like that."

Both fairies took to the air as the bells rang for the end of the match. They looked skyward to see who had won. A silver star glittered above the ring.

"It's us," cried Bella. "We've done it."

A cheer rang out from their supporters when the score went up. The Stars had achieved

Bugs and Butterflies

fifty-one bugs and butterflies! It was a spectacular win. Musk Mallow and her team gave three cheers for the losers, who had scored a respectable thirty-two.

"You played wonderfully, all of you," Musk Mallow said. "I'm bursting with pride. I couldn't have wished for a better team."

Linnet put her arm around Lila's shoulders and echoed Musk Mallow's words.

"I couldn't have wished for a better player to take my place," she said. Lila blushed her deepest purple and smiled her broadest smile. Meggie rushed over and hugged both of them and Mistress Pipit, who had been watching carefully, made a special point of saying well done, as did Mistress Arum, the referee.

From the far side of the ring Captain Klop gave Lila a nod and a slow wink. Lila smiled back, glad he'd been watching too.

Everyone returned to the refectory for the

Winners and Losers

after-match celebrations. All the Star and Sun players were there and Fairy Flowerdew, the school cook, had made them a feast of chocolate and violet brownies and a great plateful of beechnut and honey muffins. Mugs of elderflower and honey juice quenched their thirsts.

"I couldn't have been caught by a worthier opponent," Marigold told Lila with a smile. "But I'm going to remember that little trick. I warn you, Lilac Blossom, you won't get me out like that again. I'm calling it the spinning-top maneuver. So watch out!"

There was so much to explain and talk about that it wasn't until nearly bedtime that Lila saw Bee Balm again. Their eyes met and the Princess raised her royal hand.

"Ah, Lilac Blossom, I want you to know I'm giving up Bugs and Butterflies to concentrate on my studies. It's a frivolous game. I can't think why I ever wanted to play it in the first place."

Bugs and Butterflies

"What you mean is that you've been dropped from the team," said Bella, coming over. "I wonder why? Perhaps for being unable to somersault? Or maybe for hiding in the undergrowth?"

"If you say one more word I will tell the Lord Chamberlain what that dragon did to my shoes."

"Big threat," said Bella. "You wouldn't dare. Not when we all know how badly you play Bugs and Butterflies without the shoes. You are the meanest, most self-centered fairy I have ever met. If you ever become Queen I will leave the kingdom."

"*When* I become Queen," Bee Balm snapped back, eyes blazing. "And it'll be good riddance."

"Stop it, you two," said Lila.

"Oh, Miss Pots-and-Pans, I wondered when you were going to join in."

"Don't bother with her, Lila," Bella said, taking Lila's arm and glaring at the Princess. "She's not worth it."

Winners and Losers

Bee Balm glared back, took Sea Holly's arm and marched off.

"Well, what do you know," said Meggie. "I think we're back where we started."

"Better that than having false friends," Bella said.

"Yes, I agree. It's better to know where we stand," said Lila, stopping to help herself to another chocolate and violet brownie. As she did so her school bracelet slid up her arm. She smiled at the little unicorn, then took a big chocolaty bite.

Later, lying in bed, tired but happy, Lila gently stroked the little silver unicorn with her finger.

"Winning at Bugs and Butterflies was the best," she whispered to him. "But when will you come to life? Please, can it be soon?"

She was certain the little unicorn gave her finger a nudge and she snuggled under the covers dreamily thinking of the letter she

Bugs and Butterflies

was going to write to Cook and Mip telling them all about playing for the Star Clan team – and winning. She yawned, tired after such an exciting day and very soon was fast asleep.

Join Lila and her friends
for more magical adventures at

Silverlake Fairy School

www.silverlakefairyschool.com

Unicorn Dreams

Lila longs to go to Silverlake Fairy School to learn about wands, charms and fairy magic – but spoiled Princess Bee Balm is set on ruining Lila's chances! Luckily nothing can stop Lila from following her dreams...

Wands and Charms

It's Lila's first day at Silverlake Fairy School, and she's delighted to receive her first fairy charm and her own wand. But Lila quickly ends up breaking the school rules when bossy Princess Bee Balm gets her into trouble. Could Lila's school days be numbered...?

Ready to Fly

Lila and her friends love learning to fly at Silverlake Fairy School. Their lessons in the Flutter Tower are a little scary but fantastic fun. Then someone plays a trick on Lila and she's grounded. Only Princess Bee Balm would be so mean. But how can Lila prove it?

Stardust Surprise

Stardust is the most magical element in the
fairy world. Although the fairies are allowed to
experiment with it in lessons, stardust is so powerful
that they are forbidden to use it by themselves.
But Princess Bee Balm will stop at nothing
to boost her magic...

Dancing Magic

It's the beginning of winter at Silverlake Fairy
School, and Lila and her friends are practicing to
put on a spectacular show. There's a wonderful
surprise in store for Lila too – one she didn't
dare dream was possible!

About the Author

Elizabeth Lindsay trained as a drama teacher before becoming a puppeteer on children's television. Elizabeth has published over thirty books, as well as writing numerous radio and television scripts including episodes of *The Hoobs*. Elizabeth dreams up adventures for Lilac Blossom from her attic in Gloucestershire, where she enjoys fairytale views down to the River Severn valley. If Elizabeth could go to Silverlake Fairy School, she would like a silver wand with a star at its tip, as she'd hope to be with Lila in the Star Clan. Like Lila, Elizabeth's favorite color is purple.